CONTENTS

Bolton
Council

Please return/ renew this item
by the last date shown.
Books can also be renewed at
www.bolton.gov.uk/libraries

For Pablo. But not to eat.

First published in 2020 in Great Britain by
Barrington Stoke Ltd
18 Walker Street, Edinburgh, EH3 7LP

www.barringtonstoke.co.uk

Text © 2020 Jonathan Meres
Illustrations © 2020 Katy Halford

A CIP catalogue record for this book is available
from the British Library upon request

ISBN: 978-1-78112-953-1

Printed by Hussar Books, Poland

CHAPTER 1
New Boy

The day began like every other day began at Wigley Primary.

"Good morning, everyone!" said Mr Reed.

"Gooooooood moooooooooorning, Mis-ter Reeeeeeeeeeeeeeeed!" sang the children. They stretched out each word so that they nearly ran out of breath.

Mr Reed smiled. Because only he knew what he was about to say next. And he knew that what he was about to say next would make everyone very excited.

"I have something important to tell you," said Mr Reed.

Outside, a crow cawed and a car tooted its horn. But inside, everything suddenly went very quiet. Everyone was wondering what Mr Reed would say.

"Is it your birthday, Mr Reed?" said Sol.

"No, Sol," said Mr Reed. "It's not my birthday. But that's a very good guess."

Sol looked quite pleased with himself, even though he wasn't right.

"Is it macaroni cheese for lunch, Mr Reed?" said Shakira.

"No, Shakira," said Mr Reed. "It's even *more* special than that."

"Whoa!" said Shakira, who couldn't think of *anything* more special than macaroni cheese. Especially if it came with garlic bread and a little bit of salad on the side.

"Yes, Nora?" said Mr Reed, spotting that Nora had put her hand up.

"Has a new day of the week been invented?" said Nora.

"Don't be so *stupid*!" said a voice before Mr Reed had a chance to answer.

"Now, now, Josh," said Mr Reed. "There's no need for that. That was a brilliant guess, Nora."

Nora grinned.

"Sorry, Nora," said Josh. But he didn't sound very sorry.

"That's OK," said Nora.

"Now," said Mr Reed. "Is everyone listening?"

Everybody nodded. You could tell that they were all desperate to know what Mr Reed was going to tell them.

"Excellent," said Mr Reed. "Because today we are welcoming a new member of class!"

Everyone gasped. There hadn't been a new member of class since Abdul arrived. And that was *ages* ago.

"Are you ready to meet him?" said Mr Reed.

There was another gasp. So it was a boy, not a girl. But what would he be like? Everyone began to wonder.

Sol wondered how old he would be. Shakira wondered if he would like macaroni cheese. Nora wondered if he would like science and inventing stuff, like she did. Josh wondered if he would be good at football, like he was.

"Well?" said Mr Reed. "Are you ready?"

"Yes, Mis-ter Reeeeeeeeeeeeeed!" sang the children all together.

"You must be nice and quiet when I bring him in," said Mr Reed. "He's a little bit shy."

"Like you," Callum whispered to Lou. But Lou didn't say anything. Because it was true. She was a bit shy.

"Will you all be nice and quiet?" said Mr Reed.

"Yes, Mis-ter Reeeeeeeeeeeeeed!" sang everyone together. But they sang it very quietly.

"Good," said Mr Reed as he walked out of the classroom. "I'll be back in a minute."

Everyone waited. But no one said anything. There were too many questions spinning around in their heads. What would the new member of the class look like? What would his name be? Who would he sit next to?

But there was one question *no one* had thought to ask. How many *legs* would their new classmate have?

"Boys and girls," said Mr Reed as he came back into the room carrying a small dog, "I'd like you all to meet Noodle."

"WOOF! WOOF! WOOF!" said the dog, before looking up at Mr Reed and licking his face.

CHAPTER 2
Meet Noodle

There was no need for Mr Reed to tell everyone to be quiet. The moment he'd walked back into the class holding Noodle in his arms like a baby, everyone was silent. No one could believe what they were looking at. Could this *really* be the new member of the class? A dog? An actual real-life *dog*? And not just any old dog. The cutest-looking dog, with shaggy golden curls, a black button nose and a bushy tail, just like a fox. It was the biggest surprise ever.

Abdul was the first person to say something.

"He's beautiful," he said.

"I love him," said Nora.

"He looks like a teddy bear," said Callum.

"What kind of dog is he, Mr Reed?" asked Sol.

"Ah, now that's a good question, Sol," said Mr Reed as he put Noodle down on the floor. "He's some kind of doodle."

Sol didn't understand.

"Some kind of *doodle?*" he said. "What does that mean?"

"It means he's a cross," said Mr Reed.

"He doesn't look very cross to me," said Josh as Noodle suddenly began whizzing around, sniffing everything.

Mr Reed laughed.

"What I mean," he said, "is that he's a bit of a mixture."

"Like a cheese board?" said Shakira.

"What are you on about, Shakira?" said Josh.

"Like a cheese board in a fancy restaurant," Shakira told him. "When you ask for cheese in a restaurant, you don't just get *one* kind of cheese. You get a *mixture.*"

"Well done, Shakira!" said Mr Reed. "That's a very good analogy!"

Everyone looked puzzled. They had no idea what an analogy was.

"Analogy is just another word for how something can be like something else," said Mr Reed.

"So what's he a mixture of?" said Callum as Noodle started to sniff around his chair.

"I'm not sure," said Mr Reed. "Possibly a Poodle and a Labrador?"

"That would mean he's a Labradoodle," said Nora, who knew about these things.

"Yeah, or a *Poodor*," grinned Sol, because that sounded rude.

"A *Poodor*?" said Josh. "Yuk! That's *disgusting*!"

Noodle couldn't care less what kind of dog he was. He was much more interested in sniffing things. And right now he was sniffing Shakira's bag.

"Oi!" giggled Shakira when she noticed. "Get your furry snout out!"

Noodle got his snout out of Shakira's bag. But only after he'd grabbed her pencil case and run off with it.

The others all laughed as Shakira chased Noodle around the classroom. She caught him at last and after a few seconds got him to drop the pencil case.

"Aw, yuk!" she wailed. "It's all soggy!"

"Is he your dog, Mr Reed?" said Marty. He hadn't said anything yet. Which was odd, because he was normally very chatty. But something was bothering him.

"No," said Mr Reed. "I've just borrowed him for a while."

Marty frowned.

"*Borrowed* him?" he said.

Mr Reed nodded.

"From an elderly aunt of mine. She's had to go into a nursing home."

"Cool!" said Sol.

Everyone suddenly turned and stared at Sol.

"I didn't mean it was cool that your aunt had gone into a nursing home, Mr Reed!" said Sol when he worked out why everyone was staring. "I meant it was cool that you've borrowed Noodle!"

Mr Reed smiled.

"It's OK, Sol," he said. "I know what you meant."

Sol smiled.

"Why do you ask, Marty?" said Mr Reed.

"Erm, well ..." began Marty, before stopping again.

"It's OK, Marty," said Mr Reed kindly. "You can say it."

"I don't like dogs," muttered Marty.

"Oh, really?" said Mr Reed. He hadn't thought there would be anyone in the class who didn't like dogs. "And why do you think that is?"

"I'm not sure," Marty said. "I think it might be because my mum doesn't like them."

"Wait," said Josh. "Your mum doesn't like dogs, so you don't either?"

"Dunno," said Marty. "Maybe."

"That's *stupid*!" sneered Josh.

"Now, now, Josh," said Mr Reed. "We can't always help the way we feel about things, can we?"

"What don't you like, Josh?" asked Nora.

Josh thought for a moment.

"Macaroni cheese," he said.

Shakira looked shocked.

"What?" she said. "You don't like macaroni cheese? Are you crazy?"

Abdul suddenly burst out laughing.

"What's so funny about that?" said Josh.

"No, look!" yelled Abdul, pointing at the ground next to Josh.

16

Josh looked down to see Noodle with one back leg lifted in the air, peeing all over the leg of his table.

"NOOOOOOOOOOOOOOO!" screamed Josh at the top of his voice.

But it was too late. Noodle was in full flow. There was no stopping him now.

The others all burst out laughing too. Even Marty thought it was funny. The only person who *didn't* think it was funny was Josh.

"Could have been worse!" grinned Sol when Noodle finished. "At least he didn't do a—"

"Thank you, Sol!" said Mr Reed, holding up a hand to interrupt.

But everyone knew what Sol had been about to say. They all laughed again. And this time even Josh thought it was funny.

CHAPTER 3
Your Attention, Please

Noodle the doodle soon got used to life at Wigley Primary. It was a very small school, with only two classrooms. So it didn't take long for Noodle to sniff everything that needed to be sniffed. But he still liked to whizz around first thing in the morning to make sure that everything was OK. It was part of his daily routine.

In many ways, Noodle really was like a new member of class. Not all ways, of course. He had to learn to go outside when he needed the toilet, instead of peeing on someone's table leg.

And when it came to lunchtime, he ate from a bowl on the ground instead of sitting at a table with the boys and girls. Which is what he really wanted to do.

But apart from that, he was treated just like everyone else. And just like everyone else, Noodle liked some things better than others. He wasn't very interested in learning about science or other countries. But he liked to sing along with the class when Mr Reed played the piano. And he loved playing games. Especially if it was a game where he could chase after a ball or catch things in his mouth. He liked art too, as long as he could dip his paws in paint and make a mess. Because when it came to making a mess, Noodle was the best.

Sometimes Noodle got a bit too excited, which made him feel sleepy. When that happened, he liked to curl up on a beanbag and listen to someone read a story. It didn't matter what kind of story. It could be funny or scary.

Magical or exciting. Noodle just loved to listen.
And the person he loved to listen to the most was
Lou. Lou had a soft quiet voice. It made Noodle
feel calm. And it made Lou feel nice too. Because
she was very shy. When she read to Noodle, she
pretended that no one else could hear.

Sometimes Noodle did odd jobs, like picking things up from the floor and putting them in the bin. Sometimes he helped with the recycling. Once, he helped Marty deliver a note to Miss Smith in the Infants class. Or rather, Marty helped Noodle. Either way, the note ended up getting all soggy and Miss Smith couldn't read it. So they didn't do that again.

Life went on as normal at Wigley Primary. The days began the same as they always began. Well, *almost* the same.

"Good morning, everyone!" said Mr Reed a few weeks later.

"Gooooooood mooooooooorning, Mis-ter Reeeeeeeeeeeeeeeed!" sang the children. They stretched out each word until they nearly ran out of breath.

"WOOF!" said Noodle. "WOOF, WOOF, WOOF!"

"Gooooooood moooooooooooorning, Nooooooooooooooooodle the doooooooooodle!" sang the children.

Mr Reed smiled. Because only he knew what he was about to say next. And he knew that what he was about to say next would make everyone very excited.

"Your attention, please," he said. "I have something important to tell you."

Everything suddenly went very quiet. Everyone was wondering what the important something was. Even Noodle sat still and tilted his head to one side. He was wondering too.

"Is there another new member of class, Mr Reed?" asked Josh. "A hamster? Or maybe a fish?"

"No, Josh," laughed Mr Reed. "Not this time."

"Is it your birthday, Mr Reed?" said Sol.

"No, Sol," said Mr Reed. "It's still not my birthday. But I'll be sure to let you know when it is."

"Is it *Noodle's* birthday, Mr Reed?" said Abdul.

Mr Reed smiled.

"No, Abdul," he said. "It isn't Noodle's birthday, either. At least, I don't think it is."

"Is it macaroni cheese for lunch, Mr Reed?" said Shakira.

"No, Shakira," said Mr Reed. "I'm afraid it isn't."

"Thank goodness for that," muttered Josh to himself.

"Have scientists discovered a new kind of penguin, Mr Reed?" said Nora.

"No, Nora," said Mr Reed kindly. "But that's a very good guess."

Everyone waited for Mr Reed to carry on. And after a few more seconds, he did.

"There will be no school next Friday."

Everything suddenly went very quiet again. Had Mr Reed *really* just said what they *thought* he'd said? What did he mean, *no school*?

"Is it being knocked down?" asked Sol.

Mr Reed smiled.

"No, Sol," he said. "The school's not being knocked down."

"Is it going to be zapped by aliens and taken somewhere else?" said Nora.

Mr Reed laughed.

"No, Nora," he said. "But *we're* being taken somewhere else."

Abdul gasped.

"By *aliens?*"

"No, Abdul," said Mr Reed. "By your dad."

"Oh," said Abdul.

Abdul's dad drove a bus. Which meant that they must be going on a school trip.

"Where to, Mr Reed?" asked Callum.

Mr Reed didn't answer right away. The children got more and more excited as they waited.

"We're going to the seaside," said Mr Reed at last.

No one said anything. No one dared to say anything in case they were dreaming.

"Well?" said Mr Reed at last. "Are you happy?"

"YEEEEEEEEEEEEEEEEEEEEEEEEEAAAAAAA-AAAAHHHHHHHHHHH!" yelled the whole class together.

"Excellent!" said Mr Reed.

And then the questions began.

"Do we need to bring pyjamas?" asked Sol.

"No, we don't need to bring pyjamas, Sol!" laughed Mr Reed. "It's just a day trip!"

"What about food?" asked Shakira.

"Yes, Shakira," Mr Reed replied. "You definitely need to bring food."

"Can I bring my football?" asked Josh.

"Of course you can, Josh!" said Mr Reed.

"But ..." began Marty, then he stopped.

Mr Reed turned to Marty.

"What's the matter, Marty?"

"Who's going to look after Noodle?" Marty asked.

Mr Reed smiled.

"Oh, don't worry about Noodle, Marty," he said. "He's coming too!"

"YEEEEEEEEEEEEEEEEEEEEAAAAAAAAAAA-AAHHHHHHHH!" yelled everyone again.

"WOOF!" said Noodle the doodle. "WOOF! WOOF! WOOF! WOOF! WOOF!"

CHAPTER 4
Are We There Yet?

The next Friday was bright and clear. Perfect weather for a trip to the seaside.

By the time the bus arrived outside the gates of Wigley Primary, the pupils were buzzing with excitement. They crowded round the door of the bus like a swarm of bees. When the door whooshed open, they rushed up the steps.

"Hello, Mr Patel," said Josh to the driver.

"Good morning, Josh," replied Mr Patel.

"Hello, Mr Patel," said Nora.

"Good morning, Nora," said Mr Patel. "How are you?"

"Very well, thank you," replied Nora as she made her way down the bus.

"Morning, Abdul's dad," grinned Sol. Because that's what he always called Mr Patel.

"Morning, Sol!" laughed Mr Patel, who always found it funny.

"Hello, Dad," said Abdul.

"Hello, son," Mr Patel replied. "Did you remember to brush your teeth?"

"Dad!" hissed Abdul. "You're embarrassing me!"

"That's what dads do," Mr Patel replied. "It's their job."

Abdul opened his mouth to say something else, but, before he could, Noodle bounded up the steps, with Mr Reed just behind him.

"Ah, so this is the famous Noodle, is it?" said Mr Patel.

"WOOF!" said Noodle, when he heard Mr Patel say his name.

"Abdul's told me all about you," Mr Patel went on. He ruffled Noodle's fur and patted him on the back. "Yes, he has!"

"WOOF!" said Noodle again, who loved being ruffled and patted.

Mr Reed stood at the front of the bus and made everyone shush. "Right, everybody," he said, "remember what we talked about? Best behaviour?"

"YEEEEEEEES, Mis-ter REEEEEEEEEEEEEED!" sang all the pupils together.

"Seatbelts on?" said Mr Reed.

"YEEEEEEEES, Mis-ter REEEEEEEEEEEEED!" sang the pupils again.

"Excellent!" said Mr Reed, sitting on the front seat with Noodle by his feet. "In that case, Mr Patel, let's go!"

"YEEEEEEEEEEEAAAAAAAAAAAAAHHHHHH!" yelled everyone at the tops of their voices.

"WOOF!" said Noodle. "WOOF! WOOF! WOOF! WOOF!"

The door whooshed closed again and, with a toot of the horn, the bus set off.

"Are we there yet, Abdul's dad?" yelled Sol before they'd even got to the end of the street. Everybody laughed. Even Abdul.

A few minutes later, they'd left the village behind and were driving along country roads.

Josh looked out the window.

"I spy, with my little eye," he said, "something beginning with … 'w'."

"Window," said Nora straight away.

Josh was amazed.

"How did you know that?" he said.

"Just did," said Nora with a shrug of her shoulders. "I spy, with *my* little eye, something beginning with ... 'e'."

Josh pulled a face. He couldn't see anything beginning with 'e'.

"Elephant?" he said hopefully.

"*Elephant?*" said Nora.

"OK, what is it then?" asked Josh.

"Everything," said Nora.

Meanwhile, Shakira had already opened her lunchbox and was busy tucking into a cheese and tomato sandwich.

"Yum," she said between mouthfuls.

"STOP THE BUS I NEED A WEE WEE!" sang Callum from the back of the bus.

Mr Reed turned around.

"Do you *really* need a wee wee, Callum?" he asked.

"No, not really, Mr Reed," said Callum.

"Does *anybody* need a wee wee?" asked Mr Reed, addressing the whole bus. "If you do, please put your hand up now."

But nobody put their hand up.

"Excellent," said Mr Reed, looking down at his feet. "And how about you, Noodle? Do *you* need a wee wee?"

But Noodle was already fast asleep.

CHAPTER 5
Crazy Dog

They arrived at Snoreham-on-Sea just after eleven o'clock. It was a beautiful day. The sun was shining. The sky was blue. There wasn't a cloud in sight. The sea was as smooth as glass. A sailing boat was slowly making its way from one side of the horizon to the other.

But Noodle the doodle couldn't care less about any of that stuff. There were so many new things to sniff. And as soon as he'd hopped down from the bus and peed on the nearest lamp post, he started to whizz about.

"Whoa!" cried Mr Reed. He gave Noodle's lead a tug. "Slow down, boy! Where's the fire?"

But there was no fire. Noodle was just in a hurry to explore everything. It didn't matter if they were going to stay for five minutes or five weeks. He was going to whizz around at a million miles an hour anyway.

As the name suggested, Snoreham-on-Sea was a sleepy little place. There were no amusement arcades. There was no funfair. There was no pier sticking out into the sea. The most exciting thing by far was the crazy golf. Noodle must have thought so too. He tugged hard on his lead and yanked Mr Reed onto the course.

"Why's it called crazy golf?" said Callum.

"Because you'd have to be crazy not to want to play!" laughed Sol.

"Can we play, Mr Reed?" said Josh.

"Ooh, yes, can we, Mr Reed?" pleaded Shakira. "Can we, can we, can we, pleeeeeeeeeeeease?"

Mr Reed thought for a second.

"Hmm," he said. "What do the rest of you think? Would you all like to play crazy golf too?"

"YEEEEEEEEEEEEEEEAAAAAAAAAAAHHHH-HHHHHH!" yelled everyone else. Well, *almost* everyone else. Marty didn't yell. He looked a bit worried. When all the others rushed off to find clubs and balls, he stayed behind at the gate.

"Something wrong, Marty?" said Mr Reed.

"I don't know how to play," said Marty in a small, sad voice. "I've never done it before."

Mr Reed smiled kindly.

"Don't worry," he said. "Neither have I!"

Marty looked at Mr Reed for a moment. He didn't know if Mr Reed was joking.

"Really?" said Marty. "You're not just saying that to make me feel better?"

"I promise you, Marty," he said. "I've never played crazy golf in my life. And I'm a little bit older than you!"

Marty thought for a moment. Because Mr Reed wasn't just a *little* bit older than Marty. He was a *lot* older.

"So this will be the first time for both of us then," said Marty.

"WOOF!" said Noodle. "WOOF! WOOF! WOOF!"

Mr Reed looked at Noodle.

"What's that, boy?" he said.

"He says it's going to be the first time for him too," said Marty.

Mr Reed laughed.

"Do you know something, Marty? I think you might be right. Come on. Let's give it a go, shall we?"

The others were already having great fun. Josh was trying to hit his golf ball over a little bridge. Shakira was aiming for the door of a tiny windmill. Meanwhile, Lou was trying to get her ball to roll through a tunnel and drop into a hole on the other side.

But Noodle the doodle had other ideas. He thought that it would be much more exciting to chase after everybody's balls and run off with them in his mouth. So that's what he did.

It was funny the first time. Everybody laughed. It was funny the second time too. So everybody laughed again. But when Noodle grabbed someone's ball for the sixth time and zoomed off with it, no one thought it was funny any more. There was huffing and puffing. There were mumblings and grumblings. When it happened for the tenth time, no one at all was laughing. Even Sol was getting annoyed. And Sol hardly ever got annoyed about anything.

"DROP IT, NOODLE!" yelled Sol.

"COME BACK, NOODLE!" yelled Callum.

"HERE, BOY!" yelled Shakira.

The only trouble was that by now Noodle thought that chasing golf balls around the crazy golf course was the best game ever. Even better than chasing after sticks. Or squirrels. Or running around in circles trying to catch his own tail.

And the more fuss that people made, the more he wanted to do it. Nothing was going to stop him. They could yell and shout as much as they liked. Noodle was just going to keep on doing it. And doing it. And doing it. Until all of a sudden, he vanished.

"Where's he gone?" said Marty.

Everyone looked around. But Noodle was nowhere to be seen. He'd vanished into thin air.

Suddenly no one was cross any more. Everyone was worried. Everything went quiet. But not for long.

"WOOF!" said Noodle, his furry snout sticking out of the tunnel. "WOOF! WOOF! WOOF! WOOF! WOOF!"

Everyone laughed. They were so happy that Noodle was safe. How could you be cross with Noodle the doodle?

"Come here, you," said Mr Reed. "Time to get you back on your lead!"

CHAPTER 6

Come Back With That Sausage!

By now it was nearly time for lunch. And there was only one place to have it. The beach! Everyone was very excited as they sat down on the sand to open their lunchboxes. Well, *nearly* everyone. Shakira wasn't excited. She was actually feeling a bit fed up.

"What's the matter, Shakira?" said Mr Reed, who could always tell when someone was feeling bad.

For a moment it looked as if Shakira was about to cry.

"I've eaten my lunch already," she said. Not only did Shakira *look* sad but she *sounded* sad too.

"Oh dear," said Mr Reed. "What are we going to do about that, I wonder?"

"You can have some of mine, Shakira," said Sol.

"Really?" said Shakira. She wondered if Sol was being serious or not. It was sometimes hard to tell.

"Really," said Sol, nodding and holding out a banana. "Here. Take this."

Shakira smiled.

"Thank you," she said.

"Yes, thank you, Sol," said Mr Reed. "That really is very kind of you."

Sol grinned.

"That's OK," he said. "I don't even like bananas."

"You can have one of my sandwiches if you like, Shakira," said Lou softly. "They're cheese and tomato."

Shakira's face lit up. "Cheese and tomato?" she said. "Thanks, Lou!"

"Yes, thank you, Lou!" said Mr Reed. "That's very kind of you too."

Lou smiled shyly.

"That's OK," she said. "I've got loads. My dad always makes too many."

"Seriously?" said Sol. "In that case, can I have one?"

"What's the magic word, Sol?" said Mr Reed in a strict voice.

Sol thought for a moment.

"Abracadabra?" he grinned. And everyone laughed.

Noodle had been dozing until now. Worn out from all the running around, he needed a rest. But as Lou handed a sandwich to Sol, Noodle suddenly jumped up into the air and made a grab for it. He missed, but Lou dropped the sandwich. Luckily, Sol snatched it from the ground a split second before Noodle could get hold of it.

"Oh no!" cried Lou. "Now it's covered in sand!"

"Doesn't matter," grinned Sol. "It *is* a *sand*wich, after all!"

Josh groaned.

"That's a terrible joke, Sol," he said.

"Would you like a veggie sausage, Shakira?" Nora asked.

Shakira turned to see Nora holding up a sausage. But before she could answer, Noodle the doodle suddenly jumped up into the air again.

This time he got what he wanted. In the blink of an eye, he'd grabbed Nora's veggie sausage and was zooming along the beach with it.

"OI!" yelled Nora. "COME BACK WITH THAT SAUSAGE!"

Callum giggled.

"Sorry, Nora," he said, "but that's the funniest thing I've ever heard!"

Nora frowned. She didn't think it was very funny at all.

"Sorry, Nora," grinned Abdul. "But it was actually quite funny."

"Suppose so," Nora mumbled.

"Have you got another one, please?" Shakira asked Nora.

"Another sausage?" Nora replied.

Shakira nodded.

"I'm afraid not," said Nora. "That was my last one."

"That was your last sausage?" said Shakira, as if she couldn't believe what she'd just heard.

Callum couldn't help giggling again.

"What's so funny about that?" said Shakira.

"Look!" said Josh before Callum could answer.

Noodle was trotting back towards them. He was licking his lips. The veggie sausage was nowhere to be seen.

Mr Reed looked at him for a moment. He was beginning to think that bringing Noodle the doodle to the seaside had been a bad idea.

"Have you got something to say?" said Mr Reed in a cross voice.

"WOOF!" said Noodle, his tail wagging like an out-of-control windscreen wiper. "WOOF! WOOF! WOOF!"

CHAPTER 7
Ta Da!

By the time everyone had eaten their lunch, it was low tide. This meant that the sea was far away. But that was good news. Because now the beach was nice and big.

"Who wants to play football?" asked Josh, bouncing his ball on the sand and catching it again.

"Me!" said Callum.

"Me!" said Abdul.

"WOOF!" said Noodle. "WOOF! WOOF! WOOF! WOOF!"

Josh laughed and bent down to give Noodle a tickle behind his ears.

"Do you want to play football too, boy?" he said.

"WOOF!" said Noodle, wagging his tail like crazy. "WOOF! WOOF! WOOF!"

"Can I play?" said Lou in a very quiet voice.

Josh turned to Lou. He had a puzzled look on his face.

"But ..." he began.

"What?" said Lou. "I'm a *girl*?"

"No!" said Josh.

"Well, what then?" said Lou.

"I just didn't know you liked football, that's all," said Josh. "You should have said something before."

"I did," said Lou. "You probably didn't hear me."

Josh smiled. Lou was right. She did have a quiet voice.

"I like it when you read to Noodle," he said.

"Pardon?" said Lou.

"Nothing," said Josh, setting off after the others. "Come on. Let's go. You can be on my side, if you want."

"Cool," said Lou.

"Hurry up, you two!" called Abdul.

"All right, all right!" yelled Josh. He kicked the ball high into the air and ran after it. "We're coming!"

"So," said Mr Reed, watching as Josh and the others got smaller and smaller. "What are the rest of us going to do?"

"Ooh, I've got an idea, Mr Reed!" said Nora.

"Ooooh!" said Sol, trying to sound like Nora. "I've got an idea, Mr Reed!"

"Now, now, Sol," said Mr Reed. "There's no need for that."

"Well, I bet it's a *rubbish* idea," said Sol.

Shakira looked hard at Sol. Just because he'd given her his banana didn't mean that she couldn't be cross with him.

"Don't be so rotten, Sol!" said Shakira.

"Shakira's absolutely right, Sol," said Mr Reed. "Let's find out what Nora's got to say first, shall we?"

Shakira stuck her tongue out at Sol. Sol pulled a funny face at Shakira.

"Well, Nora?" said Mr Reed. "What's your idea?"

"I thought we could build a sandcastle," said Nora.

Everyone turned and looked at Nora. Sol was the first to speak.

"Whoa!" he said. "That's a *fantastic* idea, Nora! I'm sorry I was mean to you."

Nora smiled.

"Thank you," she said.

"It is actually a really brilliant idea," said Shakira. "Let's build a *massive* one!"

"Yeah!" said Sol. "Like that big fancy place in India that looks like a Christmas cake. Oh, you know. What's it called?"

"The Taj Mahal?" said Nora.

"That's it!" said Sol. "The Taj Mahal!"

Mr Reed smiled at Nora.

"Well done, Nora," he said. "Excellent general knowledge."

Nora looked pleased with herself.

"But ..." began Marty.

"What is it, Marty?" said Mr Reed.

"How can we build a sandcastle?" Marty went on. "We don't have any buckets and spades."

It was a good point. They didn't have any buckets and spades. Or at least, they didn't *think* they had.

"Did someone say we needed buckets and spades?" said a voice behind them.

They all turned around and there was Mr Patel walking down onto the beach. And he was carrying a big bag.

"Well," he said as he got closer. "Is someone going to ask me what's in the bag?"

"What's in the bag, Mr Patel?" said Shakira.

Mr Patel turned the bag upside down so everything inside tipped out onto the sand.

"TA-DA!" he boomed.

Marty gasped.

"Buckets and spades?" he said.

"That's amazing!" laughed Sol.

"Well?" said Mr Reed. "What are we waiting for? Let's get cracking!"

"Yes," said Nora. "Before the tide comes in and washes it away!"

"That's a very good point, Nora," said Mr Reed.

"Are you going to help build the sandcastle, Abdul's dad?" asked Sol.

Mr Patel grinned from ear to ear.

"Just try and stop me!" he said.

But before they could start digging, someone shouted, "MIND YOUR HEADS!"

A second later, the football flew past and only just missed Mr Patel's head. A few moments after that, Noodle flew past, chasing after the football. A few moments after *that*, Josh, Callum, Abdul and Lou all flew past, chasing after Noodle.

"LEAVE IT, NOODLE!" yelled Josh at the top of his voice. "THAT'S MY BEST BALL!"

But by now Noodle the doodle was just a tiny dot in the distance.

CHAPTER 8
Oops!

Josh was a fast runner. Callum, Abdul and Lou were all quite fast too. But none of them were as fast as Noodle. And Nora's veggie sausage had given Noodle the doodle extra energy, so he zoomed along the beach like a furry four-legged rocket. The only reason the children caught up with him at last was because Noodle stopped to scratch himself. But by then it was too late.

"Oh no," wailed Josh.

"What's the matter?" puffed Lou.

"He's burst my ball!" said Josh.

"Oops," puffed Abdul as he and Callum caught up with Josh and Lou.

Josh looked at Abdul and frowned.

"What do you mean, 'Oops'?" he said.

"Well, it's no big deal," said Abdul.

"Yeah," agreed Callum. "It's just a ball."

"Just a ball?" Josh squeaked. "My nan gave it to me for my birthday!"

"Oh, I see," said Callum. "I didn't know that. Sorry, Josh."

Josh looked down at Noodle.

"Bad dog," he said as he grabbed the burst ball.

"It's not Noodle's fault," said Lou. "He didn't know it was special."

"I think he's upset," said Abdul.

"Well, of *course* I'm upset!" said Josh. "Wouldn't *you* be?"

Abdul was puzzled.

"What?" he said. "No, I didn't mean *you*, Josh. I meant *Noodle*! Look."

Josh looked. By now, Noodle was stretched out on the sand. His nose was resting between his front paws. He was gazing up at everybody with his big brown eyes.

"I think he's just tired after all that chasing," said Lou. She sat down on the sand next to Noodle. "I'm going to stay with him for a bit."

"Whatever," said Josh, and set off back towards the others.

"See you later, Lou," said Abdul as he and Callum set off as well.

"It's OK, Noodle," said Lou as she watched them go. "It's just a silly ball. He can get another one."

Noodle rolled over so that Lou could tickle his tummy. He didn't look at all upset.

CHAPTER 9
Lost and Found

By the time the footballers arrived back, the sandcastle was already beginning to take shape. The others had been very busy. Some had been digging. Others had been building. Everyone had been busy doing something.

"Wow!" said Callum. "It's massive!"

"Oh, it's not finished yet," said Marty.

"Yeah, you're going to be able to see it from space!" said Sol. "Just like the Taj Mahal!"

"You can't see the Taj Mahal from space, Sol," said Nora. "You're thinking of the Great Wall of China."

Sol frowned.

"I am?" he said.

"Can we help?" said Abdul.

"Course you can," said Shakira. "Grab a spade!"

"Yes, absolutely, Abdul!" said Mr Reed. "The more the merrier. We need to try to get it finished before the tide comes in. And then it will be time to go home. Isn't that right, Mr Patel?"

"That's right, Mr Reed!" said Mr Patel.

Josh looked a bit sad.

"Aw. Do we *have* to, Mr Reed?" he said.

Mr Reed smiled.

"Do we have to go home, Josh?"

Josh nodded.

"Yes," laughed Mr Reed. "I'm afraid we do."

"Aw," said Josh again. "It's not fair."

"How was the football?" said Mr Reed.

Josh snorted.

"Rubbish," he said. "Noodle burst the ball. Look."

Josh held the football up for Mr Reed to inspect.

"Oh," said Mr Reed. "That *is* bad luck."

Mr Patel was busy patting his trouser pockets.

"That's strange," he said as he began patting his shirt pockets and then his jacket pockets.

"What's the matter, Mr Patel?" said Mr Reed. "Have you lost something?"

Mr Patel nodded.

"Something important?" said Mr Reed, starting to get a bit worried.

Mr Patel nodded again.

"Very important, yes," he said.

Mr Reed was starting to look worried too.

"What have you lost?"

Mr Patel didn't answer straight away.

"My keys," he said.

Mr Reed looked at him for a moment.

"Your *house* keys?"

Mr Patel shook his head.

"You mean …" Mr Reed began.

Mr Patel nodded.

"The keys for the bus," he said in a quiet voice. But not quiet enough. Because everybody else heard him. And now everybody else was worried too. Without the keys to the bus, how would they get back to Wigley? Josh may have said that he wanted to stay at Snoreham-on-Sea, but even he knew that they'd have to go home in the end.

Everyone suddenly stopped building the sandcastle.

"Where did you last see them, Dad?" said Abdul.

Mr Patel gave a sigh.

"If I knew that, they wouldn't be lost, would they?" he said.

"Suppose not," said Abdul.

"Come on, guys!" said Shakira. "What are we waiting for? Let's get looking!"

"Yes," said Callum. "But where do we start?"

"Yeah," said Sol. "It's a bit like looking for a needle in a … in a … Oh, you know. A thingy."

"A haystack?" said Nora.

"That's it!" said Sol. "A haystack! Thanks, Nora."

"You're welcome," said Nora.

But before they had a chance to think where to start looking for the keys, they heard something that made them all turn around.

"NOOOOOOOOOOOOOOOOOOOOOOOOODLE!"
yelled Lou, louder than anyone had ever heard
her yell before. "NOOOOOOOOOOOOOOOOOOO!"

And they could see why Lou was yelling.
Because Noodle was heading straight towards
the sandcastle. It looked as if he was on some
kind of mission. Nothing was going to stop him
now.

They watched as Noodle the doodle took
a flying leap. It was like something out of an
action movie. Everything seemed to go into
slow motion as he shot through the air like a
missile. And then? Bullseye. He hit the target.

Straightaway, Noodle began to dig. And dig.
And dig. Faster and faster, until his paws were
just a blur and everyone got covered in sand.

"NOOOOOOOOOOOOODLE!" they all yelled.
"NOOOOOOOOOOOOOOOOOOO!"

But it was too late. The sandcastle was already beginning to crumble and collapse. At this rate, it would soon be totally destroyed. And there would be no time to make another one. Because the tide was coming back in.

"Wait a minute," said Marty.

"What is it?" said Josh.

"I think he might have found something!" Marty said.

Marty was right. Noodle had definitely found something. But what?

Josh wondered if it might be a ball.

Shakira wondered if it might be something to eat.

Nora wondered if it might be the bone of a dinosaur. A new kind of dinosaur that no one knew about yet. That would be amazing. They could call it a *doodlesaurus*!

But it turned out to be none of those things.

"MY KEYS!" boomed Mr Patel. His voice was so loud that it scared a passing seagull.

Mr Patel was right. There, dangling from Noodle's mouth, was a bunch of keys.

"You must have dropped them after lunch, Abdul's dad," said Sol.

"Yes," said Nora. "When you were tipping the buckets and spades out of the bag."

But right now, Mr Patel didn't care about how or why he'd lost the keys. All he cared about was how he was going to get them back.

Everyone was standing still, looking at Noodle. No one moved. Because they knew that if anyone tried to grab the keys, Noodle might

run off with them. Just like he ran off with
the golf balls. And Nora's veggie sausage. And
Josh's football. And if that happened, they might
never see the keys again.

"Noodle?" said Lou.

Noodle looked at Lou and tilted his head to one side. It was very cute. But no one laughed. Now was the time for cool heads.

"Drop it," said Lou. Her voice was gentle but firm.

Noodle looked at Lou. Lou looked at Noodle. The others all held their breath. It was very tense.

But then something amazing happened. Noodle dropped the keys.

"Wow!" whispered Shakira.

"Awesome!" whispered Callum.

Lou stepped forwards and picked up the keys.

"Good boy," she said, patting Noodle on the head.

Mr Reed smiled.

"Well done, Lou!" he said.

"Yes, thank you, Lou!" said Mr Patel. "You're our hero!"

"No," said Lou. Her voice was gentle but firm. "I'm not a hero. *Noodle's* a hero."

"WOOF!" said Noodle the doodle. "WOOF! WOOF! WOOF!"

And everybody laughed.

CHAPTER 10
Some Kind of Doodle

Mr Reed and Noodle were the last to get back onto the bus.

"All aboard?" Mr Patel asked.

Mr Reed nodded.

"All present and correct, Mr Patel," he said. "I checked as they were getting on."

"Marvellous," said Mr Patel, pushing a button.

The doors of the bus whooshed closed and the engine rumbled into life.

"Seatbelts on, everyone?" said Mr Reed in a loud voice.

"YEEEEEEEES, Mis-ter REEEEEEEEEEEEEEEEEEED!" sang the pupils of Wigley Primary all together.

"Excellent," said Mr Reed. "In that case, let's go, Mr Patel!"

And that was that. With a toot of the horn, they were off.

"Are we there yet, Abdul's dad?" called Sol from the back of the bus less than a minute later.

Everyone knew that Sol was going to say it. But it was still funny when he did. Because it had been such a wonderful day. They were all in a good mood. They were sad to leave

Snoreham-on-Sea. But they also couldn't wait to get home and tell everyone about everything that had happened. The crazy golf. The picnic on the beach. The sandcastle.

But most of all, they wanted to tell everyone about Noodle and how he'd found the keys. Of course, he didn't know that they were keys. He didn't know how important they were. That didn't matter. What mattered was that Noodle had saved the day.

Marty was sat next to Mr Reed at the front of the bus.

"Mr Reed?" said Marty after a little while.

"Yes, Marty?" said Mr Reed.

"I think I might have changed my mind about dogs."

"Oh, really?" said Mr Reed.

Marty nodded.

"Yes, I think I might like them now," he said.

Mr Reed smiled.

"I'm very pleased to hear it, Marty," he said.

Marty thought for a moment as the bus left the sea behind and began heading back inland.

"Mr Reed?" he said.

"Yes, Marty," said Mr Reed.

"You know you said that Noodle was some kind of doodle?" said Marty.

"That's right, Marty," said Mr Reed. "I did say that."

"Well, I know what kind of doodle he is," said Marty.

"Oh, really?" said Mr Reed.

Marty nodded.

"What kind?" said Mr Reed.

"A Superdoodle," said Marty.

Mr Reed looked at Marty.

"Do you know something, Marty?" he laughed. "I think you might be right."

Marty reached under the seat to give Noodle a tickle.

"Did you hear that, Noodle?" he said.

But Noodle didn't hear. Because Noodle the Superdoodle was already fast asleep.